THOMAS·AQUINAS·MAGUIRE

a growling place

SIMPLY READ BOOKS

First published in 2007 by Simply Read Books
www.simplyreadbooks.com

Text and Illustrations © 2007 Thomas Aquinas Maguire

Book design by
Thomas Aquinas Maguire, Dimiter Savoff and Elisa Gutiérrez

CATALOGUING IN PUBLICATION DATA

Maguire, Thomas Aquinas, 1981-
    A growling place / Thomas Aquinas Maguire, author and illustrator.
ISBN 978-1-894965-74-3
    I. Title.

PS3613.A352G76 2007   j813'.6   C2007-900739-2

10 9 8 7 6 5 4 3 2 1 • Printed in Singapore

They used their might and their bite to frighten and scare ...

...until Aril shouted, shaming them bullies!

The bears began to cry, so she calmed them down... by dressing them up!

In collars, and bowties and clever top hats,

they felt kinder and wiser and gentlemanly!

"Bullies no longer!" they sang in their merry-bear march...

...as Aril told them lazy stories of her warm-orange homeful...

...of quilts, and quiets, and goodnight tea.